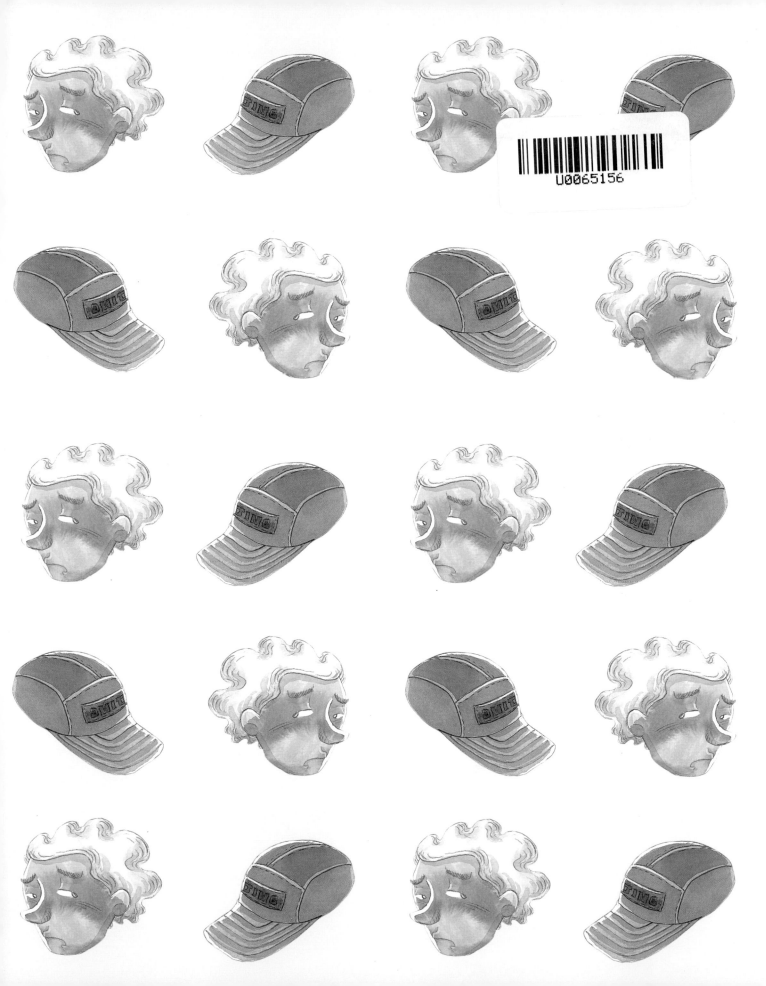

Jason's Big Secret

杰生的大秘密

Coleen Reddy　著

倪靖、郜欣、王平　繪

蘇秋華　譯

三民書局

For Mom

Thank you for everything.

獻給我的母親
　感謝您為我所做的一切

Being popular is not easy. In fact, it is a lot of hard work. The trick was — making it LOOK easy. It should not be obvious that you're trying hard. It had to look very natural.

Jason Wilson was an expert at this. He was Mr. Popular. He was King Cool. All the boys in school wanted to be like him and all the girls wanted to be near him. Jason didn't really care about good grades or sports. For Jason, being popular was the most important thing.

So on Monday morning, Jason decided that he would not go to school. He had thought about it the whole night and there was nothing else he could do. He simply could not go to school on Monday morning. Something terrible had happened on Saturday that changed everything. If he went to school looking like he did, everyone would make fun of him. He would become a geek. It would be a nightmare. NO! There was no way that he was going to school. Now he had to convince his mother.

6

It was not easy to lie to Jason's mom. He would have to be very careful. He went into the bathroom and closed the door behind him. First, he wet his face and hair so that he looked like he had a fever.

After that, he rubbed his eyes and his nose until they were red. Lastly, he put some eye drops into his eyes. That made him look like he was crying and sick.

He was ready.

He went downstairs to speak to his mom. She was in the kitchen, drinking some coffee and reading the newspaper. Jason started coughing loudly. His mom looked up.

"Jason, why aren't you dressed yet? Hurry or you'll be late for school again," she said, a little sternly.

Jason didn't say anything. Couldn't his mom see that he looked sick? He tried again. He coughed louder and longer than before. His mom was sure to notice.

"Do you have something caught in your throat?" she asked.

"Um, no. I'm not feeling well. I think that I might have a cold or something," Jason said, trying to sound sick and pitiful.

His mom got up and walked over to him. She touched his forehead.

"Well, you don't have a fever," she said.

"But I have a cough and I feel like throwing up. I don't think I can go to school today," he said.

"You don't look very sick," his mom said.

"Mom, I feel really bad," he pleaded.

Jason's mom looked unconvinced.

"This doesn't have anything to do with what happened on Saturday, does it?" she asked.

"Of course not," Jason said.

"Okay, you can stay at home today. I'll call the school and tell them you're sick," she said.

16

"Yes!" thought Jason. He didn't have to go to school. But what was he going to do the next day? What excuse would he give his mother? He had to go back to school eventually. Jason was worried; he didn't know what to do.

The next day, he pretended to be sick again but his mom knew better.

"No," she said. "There's nothing wrong with you. You're as healthy as can be. You have to go to school, so get dressed!"

Jason's mom drove him to school. In the car, Jason was feeling very nervous. As they got closer to school, his heart beat faster and faster. Finally, they were there.

He walked into school and went straight to his classroom without speaking to anyone. He just looked down and kept walking. It was going to be a long day.

Jason sat at his desk. The bell rang and the other students came in and sat down at their places. His friend David, who sat in front of him, turned around to speak to him.

"Hey, how are you? I heard you were sick yesterday. What happened?" David asked.

Jason looked down.

"It was just a cold," Jason mumbled quietly.

"What did you say?" David asked.

"It was just a cold," Jason said a little louder, but still keeping his head down.

The English teacher, Mr. Peemple, walked in and started teaching. He was a boring teacher and Jason never paid attention to him.

"Today we're going to read 'A Tale of Two Cities' by Charles Dickens. Everyone can read a page. Okay? Begin!" Mr. Peemple said.

"Oh no," thought Jason. "What am I going to do?"

The students started reading. After David read, it was Jason's turn.

He kept his head down and started reading. Well, actually, it was more like mumbling. He didn't open his mouth very wide so no one could hear what he was reading.

"Louder, please Jason. We can't hear you," said Mr. Peemple.

Jason started reading again, but still no one could hear him.

Mr. Peemple looked at Jason with a curious expression on his face.

"Are you eating anything?" Mr. Peemple asked.

"No," mumbled Jason.

"You sound like you have something in your mouth," said Mr. Peemple suspiciously. He thought Jason was chewing gum or eating candy. He hated it when students did that.

"What are you eating?" Mr. Peemple asked.

Everyone was looking at Jason now. Jason didn't say anything.

Mr. Peemple was getting very angry.

"Open your mouth now!" Mr. Peemple yelled.

Jason was turning red. He looked like a tomato. He had never been so embarrassed before.

He slowly opened his mouth. Everyone stared. Right there in Jason's mouth was his big secret. It was something he hadn't told anyone at school about. It was why he didn't want to go to school. It was his biggest fear.

BRACES. *His teeth were lined with silver braces.*

David gasped. Someone giggled.

"Oh, I see," said Mr. Peemple. The class continued reading but Jason felt that everyone was staring and laughing at him.

The bell finally rang. Jason didn't move.

David and Amy walked over to him.

"So you have braces," Amy said. Amy wore braces. When she started wearing braces a few months ago, Jason had teased and laughed at her. He had called her "Metal Mouth." After that, everyone started calling her "Metal Mouth."

"Yes," replied Jason. "I got them on Saturday." He expected Amy to laugh at him and start calling him names.

"Cool, let's go now," said Amy.

"That's all you're going to say?" said Jason.

"Of course. Did you think I was going to make fun of you the way you made fun of me? I'm not a jerk like you are," said Amy.

"I'm sorry," said Jason. "I didn't know what it's like until I had to wear braces. I'll never make fun of anyone."

Amy, David, and Jason walked to their next class together.

"There are some things you should know about braces," Amy said.

"Like what?" asked Jason.

"Don't ever eat anything sticky, like chocolate, because it will stick to your braces and that can be embarrassing. No one ever tells you that you have something stuck in your braces; they just laugh at you," Amy said.

"That's comforting," said Jason sarcastically.

"Oh, and you'll probably drool a lot more when you sleep now," said Amy with a big smile.

"You're disgusting!" said Jason. Amy and David just laughed.

杰生的大秘密

受人歡迎真不簡單，而且事實上是超累的。秘訣就在於：要裝得很輕鬆、自然，完全看不出努力的痕跡最好，要讓受歡迎看起來就像是再自然也不過的事情了。杰生‧威爾森對這方面很在行，他是個萬人迷，是酷王之王。學校裡所有男生都想向他看齊，而所有的女生都想接近他。杰生並不怎麼在意學業和運動成績。對他而言，受人歡迎才是最重要的。因此，週一一大早，杰生就打定主意不去學校。他反覆思量了一整夜，除了蹺課以外，他實在想不出別的辦法。星期六發生了一件恐怖的事情，改變了他的生活。如果星期一早上他就這個樣子去學校的話，鐵定會遭到眾人的嘲笑，成為大家眼中的怪胎，生活將會變成一場惡夢。不！他絕對不去上學。現在他得想辦法騙過他的媽媽才行。

想騙媽媽可不容易，他得步步為營。杰生走進浴室，把門關好。首先，他先用水將臉和頭髮打溼，使自己看起來像是因為發高燒而冒汗的樣子。之後，他用力搓揉自己的眼睛和鼻頭，搓得一片通紅。最後，再滴幾滴眼藥水，假裝自己因為身體不舒服而哭了。

(p.1～p.9)

準備就緒，他下樓跟媽媽說話。她人在廚房，一邊喝咖啡一邊看報。杰生開始用力咳嗽，媽媽抬起頭來看他。

「杰生，你怎麼還沒穿好衣服？快點，不然又要遲到了。」她的眼神看起來有點嚴厲。

杰生沒說話，難道媽媽看不出來他不舒服嗎？他決定再試一遍，於是再度咳嗽，而且咳得比上次更用力，也比較久。這下子他媽媽想不注意也難。

她問杰生：「你是不是被什麼東西噎住了？」

杰生故意裝出病得很嚴重很可憐的樣子，說：「沒有，我覺得不舒服，我想可能是感冒了。」

(p.11～p.13)

40

媽媽站起來，走向杰生，伸出手來摸摸他額頭的溫度。

她說：「你沒發燒嘛。」

杰生爭辯：「可是我一直在咳嗽，而且很想吐。我想我今天大概沒辦法上學了。」

媽媽又說：「可是你看起來還好嘛。」

杰生哀求她：「媽，我真的覺得很難過。」

杰生的媽媽滿臉不相信的表情。

她質疑：「你老實說是不是跟禮拜六發生的事有關？」

杰生說：「當然沒有。」

媽媽讓步了：「好吧，你今天可以待在家裡，我會打電話到學校去幫你請病假。」

杰生心裡暗想：「太棒了！」他今天不用去上學……可是明天怎麼辦？他還能編什麼藉口騙媽媽？他終究還是得上學啊。杰生很擔心，不知如何是好。

到了第二天，杰生還是裝病，可是
這次媽媽也學聰明了。

(p.15～p.18)

她說：「不行，你根本就沒事，你好得很，所以一定得去上學，趕快穿好衣服！」

杰生的媽媽開車送他去學校，杰生很緊張。距離學校愈近，心就跳得愈快。終於到了。他走進學校，沒跟任何人打招呼就直接往教室裡衝。頭壓得老低，看起來無精打采。今天將會是漫長難耐。

杰生坐在自己的座位上。上課鐘響了，其他人陸續進教室坐好。坐在杰生前面的是他的朋友大維，他轉頭跟杰生說話。

大維問：「嘿，你還好吧？聽說你昨天病了，怎麼了？」

杰生低著頭不看他，口齒不清地小聲回答：「只是感冒而已。」

大維問：「你說什麼？」

杰生稍稍提高音量，說：「我說，只是感冒。」不過他的頭還是不肯抬起來。

（p.18～p.21）

英文老師皮波先生走進來，開始上課。他一向很乏味，所以杰生從來不聽課。

皮波老師說：「今天我們來唸狄更斯的《雙城記》，每個人負責朗讀一頁。好了嗎？開始！」

杰生心想：「糟了，我該怎麼辦？」

同學開始一個接一個唸，大維唸完後，就輪到杰生了。

他還是低著頭，開始朗讀……嗯，應該說他比較像在自言自語。他的嘴巴根本沒張開，所以沒有人聽得清楚他在唸什麼。

皮波老師說：「杰生，請唸大聲點，我們聽不清楚。」

杰生再唸了一次，可是還是沒人聽得到他的聲音。

皮波老師滿臉狐疑地盯著杰生。

他問杰生：「你是不是在偷吃什麼東西？」

杰生含糊地回答：「沒有啊。」

(p.22～p.25)

皮波老師不相信：「你講話的樣子聽起來好像嘴巴裡有東西。」他以為杰生在偷嚼口香糖或吃糖果，他最討厭學生在上課的時候偷吃東西了。

皮波老師問：「你在吃什麼？」

每個人都盯著杰生看，杰生不發一語。

皮波老師生氣了，大吼一聲：「嘴巴打開！」

杰生的臉漲紅了，活像顆紅番茄。他從來沒有像現在那麼糗過，然後，慢慢地，他張開嘴。

在眾人的注視下，杰生公開了他藏在嘴裡的大祕密。他從未向學校裡的任何人提起，而這也正是他不想上學的原因。嘴巴裡的東西是他最大的恐懼——牙套。他的牙齒上多了一排銀色的牙套。

（p.25～p.29）

大維倒抽了一口氣，有人則笑了出來。

皮波老師說：「喔，我懂了。」他要班上同學接下去朗讀課文，可是杰生覺得每個人都在盯著他看，而且在笑他。下課鐘聲終於響了，杰生卻沒有動作。

大維和愛玫向他走過來。

愛玫說：「你裝了牙套。」愛玫也有戴牙套，幾個月前她剛開始戴牙套的時候，還被杰生嘲弄了一番，叫她「大鋼牙」，之後，其他人也開始「大鋼牙」、「大鋼牙」地跟著叫。

杰生回答：「對，禮拜六裝的。」他以為愛玫也會笑他，然後給他取個難聽的綽號。

（p.30～p.33）

全新的大喜故事來囉！這回大喜又將碰上什麼讓我們趕快來瞧瞧！

Anna Fienberg & Barbara Fienberg／著　Kim Gamble／繪　柯美玲‧王盟雄／譯

大喜與奇妙鐘

哎呀呀！
村裡的奇妙鐘被河盜偷走了，
聰明的大喜
能幫村民們取回奇妙鐘嗎？

大喜與大臭蟲

可惡的大巨人！
不但吃掉人家的烤豬，
還吃掉人家的兒子。
大喜有辦法將巨人趕走嗎？

大喜與魔笛

糟糕！走了一群蝗蟲，
卻來了個吹笛人，
把村裡的孩子們都帶走了。
快來瞧瞧大喜是怎麼救回他們的！

大喜與算命仙

大喜就要死翹翹了！？
這可不妙！
盧半仙提議的方法，
真的救得了大喜嗎？

大喜勇退惡魔

蜘蛛、蛇和老鼠！
惡魔們絞盡腦汁要逼大喜
說出公主的下落，
大喜要怎麼從惡魔手中逃脫呢？

大喜與寶鞋

大喜的表妹阿蓮失蹤了！
為了尋找阿蓮，
大喜穿上了飛天的寶鞋。
寶鞋究竟會帶他到哪裡去呢？

波波 唸翻天系列

你知道可愛的小兔子也會 "碎碎唸" 嗎？
波波就是這樣。
他將要告訴我們什麼有趣的故事呢？

波波的復活節／波波的西部冒險記／波波上課記
我愛你，波波／波波的下雪天／波波郊遊去
波波打球記／聖誕快樂，波波／波波的萬聖夜

共 9 本，每本均附 CD

國家圖書館出版品預行編目資料

Jason's Big Secret:杰生的大秘密 / Coleen Reddy著;
倪靖, 郜欣, 王平繪; 蘇秋華譯.－－初版一刷.－－
臺北市；三民，2002
　　面；公分--(愛閱雙語叢書. 青春記事簿系列)
中英對照
ISBN 957-14-3657-7　(平裝)

805

© Jason's Big Secret
── 杰生的大秘密

著作人　Coleen Reddy
繪　圖　倪靖　郜欣　王平
譯　者　蘇秋華
發行人　劉振強
著作財
產權人　三民書局股份有限公司
　　　　臺北市復興北路三八六號
發行所　三民書局股份有限公司
　　　　地址／臺北市復興北路三八六號
　　　　電話／二五○○六六○○
　　　　郵撥／○○○九九九八──五號
印刷所　二民書局股份有限公司
門市部　復北店／臺北市復興北路三八六號
　　　　重南店／臺北市重慶南路一段六十一號
初版一刷　西元二○○二年十一月
編　號　S 85618
定　價　新臺幣參佰伍拾元整
行政院新聞局登記證局版臺業字第○二○○號

ISBN　957-14-3657-7　(平裝)

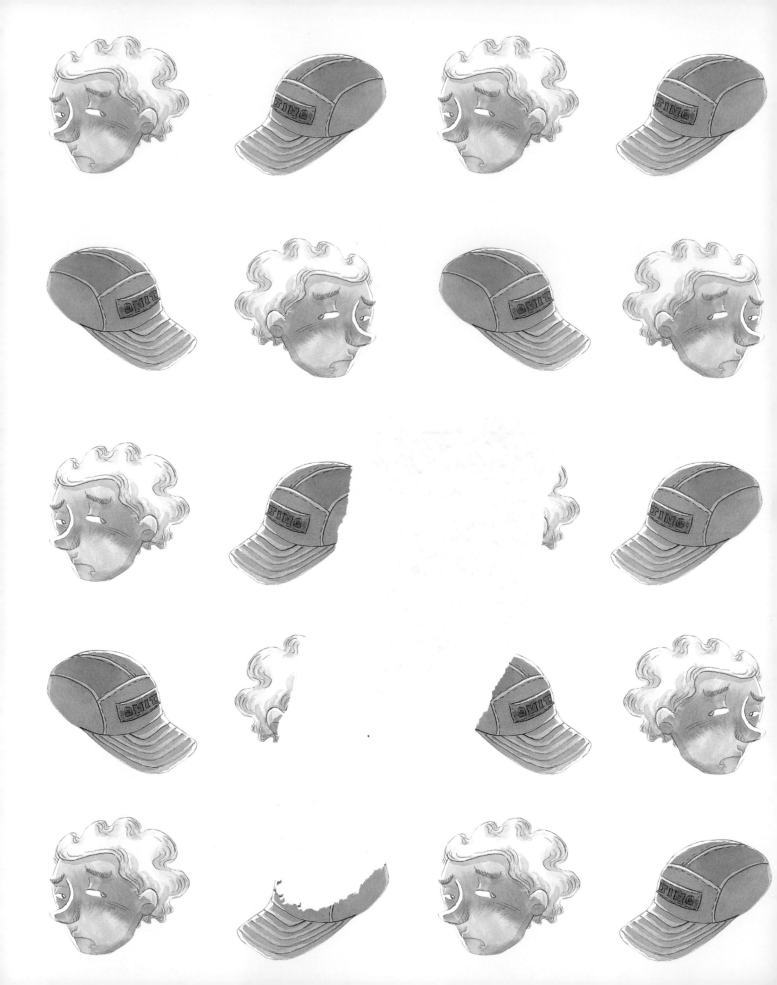